What Can I Read?

Suzanne I. Barchers

Consultants

Robert C. Calfee, Ph.D.
Stanford University

P. David Pearson, Ph.D.
University of California, Berkeley

Publishing Credits

Dona Herweck Rice, *Editor-in-Chief*
Lee Aucoin, *Creative Director*
Sharon Coan, M.S.Ed., *Project Manager*
Jamey Acosta, *Editor*
Robin Erickson, *Designer*
Cathie Lowmiller, *Illustrator*
Robin Demougeot, *Associate Art Director*
Heather Marr, *Copy Editor*
Rachelle Cracchiolo, M.S.Ed., *Publisher*

Teacher Created Materials

5301 Oceanus Drive
Huntington Beach, CA 92649-1030
http://www.tcmpub.com

ISBN 978-1-4333-2917-3

I must find a book
I can read. What
will I pick? Let me
see.

In this book, a cow is sold for beans. Jack meets a giant who is mean.

In this book, a hen plants some seeds. No one helps her water or weed.

In this book, the bed has one pea. The princess will not get much sleep.

In this book, the prince is a beast. The girl is both pretty and sweet.

In this book, the hare has fast feet. In this race, the hare still gets beat.

In this book, three
goats tramp their feet.
The troll wants to keep
the goats to eat.

In this book, two kids steal a treat. They snack on a home made of sweets.

In this book, the girl
sweeps and cleans.
But there is a prince
in her dreams.

In this book, the girl sneaks in and eats. She sits on some chairs and then sleeps.

In this book, the king and queen weep. A spell made the princess sleep.

Pete fell asleep as you can see. What book will Pete see in his dreams?

Decodable Words

and	fell	keep	pea	sneaks
beans	find	kids	Pete	spell
beast	get	king	pick	steal
beat	gets	let	plants	still
bed	goats	made	queen	sweeps
but	hare	me	race	sweet
can	has	mean	read	sweets
cleans	helps	meets	see	tramp
dreams	hen	much	seeds	treat
eat	his	must	sits	weed
eats	home	no	sleep	weep
fast	in	not	sleeps	will
feet	Jack	on	snack	

Sight Words

a	or	they
as	pretty	this
both	she	three
for	some	to
her	the	two
I	their	wants
is	them	what
of	then	who
one	there	you

Challenge Words

asleep	prince
book	princess
chairs	sold
cow	troll
giant	water
girl	

15

Extension Activities

Discussion Questions

- What are the books on each of the pages? (Page 4: *Jack and the Beanstalk*; page 5: *Little Red Hen*; page 6: *The Princess and the Pea*; page 7: *Beauty and the Beast*; page 8: *The Tortoise and the Hare*; page 9: *The Three Billy Goats Gruff*; page 10: *Hansel and Gretel*; page 11: *Cinderella*; page 12: *Goldilocks and the Three Bears*; page 13: *Sleeping Beauty*.)

- Which book do you think Pete would have chosen if he hadn't fallen asleep? Why?

- Which is your favorite story?

Exploring the Story

- Write the words *be*, *he*, and *see* on a sheet of paper. Discuss how the words either end with one *e* or two *e's*. Both patterns make the long *e* sound. What other words have this pattern? (*Bee*, *fee*, *flee*, *free*, *gee*, *glee*, *me*, *tee*, *tree*, *we*.)

- Write the word *pea*. Discuss how some words end in the letters *ea*. What other words have this pattern? (*Flea*, *plea*, *sea*, *tea*.)

- Check out as many of the books from the story as possible from the library. After reading each book, have children make a list of their favorite books.

- The story shows the covers of some books. Have children choose a story and create the front cover by writing the title on a sheet of paper and making an illustration using crayons or markers. Have children look at a variety of illustrated picture books for ideas.